READING CORNER

Camping Trip

Written by
Deborah Chancellor

Photographed by
Chris Fairclough

W
FRANKLIN WATTS
LONDON • SYDNEY

Deborah Chancellor

"When I was little, I used to make camps in the woods with my sisters. Now, I go camping with my children!"

Chris Fairclough

"I've been taking photos for books for almost 30 years and have visited 53 countries. Every day is different!"

I packed my bag to
go camping.

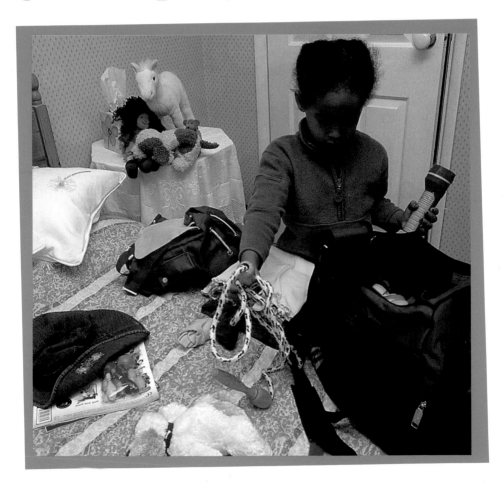

I took some
food and
drink.

My friend
Kaya came
with me.

9

Mum helped us find a dry, flat spot.

Camping Trip

A non-fiction
recount text

First published in 2004 by
Franklin Watts
96 Leonard Street
London
EC2A 4XD

Franklin Watts Australia
45–51 Huntley Street
Alexandria
NSW 2015

Text © Deborah Chancellor 2004
Photographs © Franklin Watts 2004

A CIP catalogue record for this book is available
from the British Library.

ISBN 0 7496 5310 8 (hbk)
ISBN 0 7496 5374 4 (pbk)

Series Editor: Jackie Hamley
Series Advisors: Dr Barrie Wade, Dr Hilary Minns
Design: Peter Scoulding
Photographs: Chris Fairclough

The author and publisher would especially like to thank
Sharon and Yasmin Bowen, Kaya Allen and Rosie and
Nick Gordon for giving their help and time so generously.

Printed in Hong Kong / China

We pushed
the poles into
the tent.

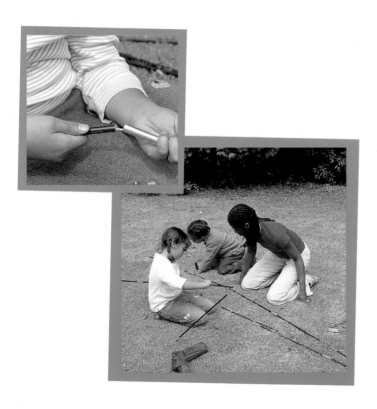

13

We lifted the tent up.

Then we put in the pegs.

We threw the cover over the top.

17

We pegged the cover down.

We pulled the ropes tight.

Then Mum
fell asleep
in the tent...

So we went to camp in my bedroom!

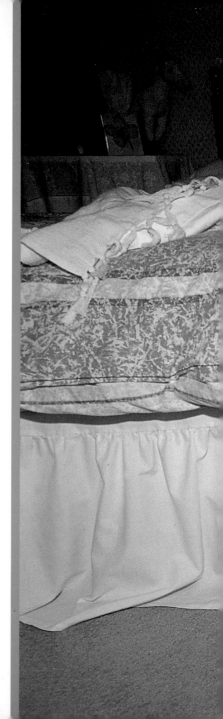